BEARS MAKE ROCK SOUP

and other stories

Paintings by Lisa Fifield

Stories by Lise Erdrich

CHILDREN'S BOOK PRESS ▪ SAN FRANCISCO, CALIFORNIA

Northern Dollmaker

Introduction

Since time began, people and animals have spoken to each other in dreams, teaching and learning from one another. They have helped each other in times of need, comforted each other when food was scarce, celebrated together in times of joy. The storytellers remember these times...

This book was made by two storytellers—artist Lisa Fifield and writer Lise Erdrich. Lisa created the paintings in this book to share her vision of people and animals helping each other. Then Lise wrote words that give voice to the stories in Lisa's paintings. Through their pictures and words, they both honor their Indian tradition in their own unique ways.

This book joins these two Native American women—one Oneida, one Ojibway—who seek to honor the bond between all humans and animals. They now pass along their vision to you, the next generation of storytellers.

Black Bear Sleeping in a Tree

It was autumn, so bears had to hurry up and get fat. Then they could squeeze into their dens and sleep all winter long.

Leaves blew off the mighty oak tree. The ground was covered with acorns. Bear ate them up, quick as he could. He looked up and saw Crow on a branch, ready to eat the very last acorn. "Haw! Haw! Haw!" laughed Crow.

Bear wanted that acorn. He climbed up after Crow to get it. But Bear was all tired out from eating. When he got up into the tree, he began to feel sleepy. "Cousin," he said to Crow, "I think I'll take a nap in your bed." He squashed himself down on Crow's nest and went to sleep.

Crow flew off hollering, "Bear is sleeping in my tree! Get him out of there! Now!"

People heard Crow and came to see what all the fuss was about. "Bear! Come down!" They poked and tickled Bear, but he paid no mind. "Our brother is a lazy fellow who only listens to his stomach," said the other bears. "Maybe he wants one last taste of summer."

So the women brought out a big bowl of berry soup. Bear woke up, his nose twitching. "What a delicious purple smell!" He slid down the tree with a great *thud*!—and joined his relatives.

"Bear is sleeping in my tree! Get him out of there! Now!"

5

The Bears that Couldn't Hibernate

One year, bears were too hungry to fall asleep.

Women came upon bears snarling in their path. "Bears, we are not your food!" they said. "We came to tell you a bedtime story. Let us go down into your warm, cozy den beneath this maple."

(Nobody wants to meet a crabby, grumpy bear. Bears need to nap, all winter long.)

Grandmother said, "We can get maple syrup for you bears, but only if you lie down and listen until you get quite sleepy. Did you forget? It's the long, slow, heavy dreaming of bears that turns the sap of the maple into our sweet medicine. When you wake up, it will be time to collect the sap in our bucket and cook it into maple sugar."

The bears began to yawn as the women told the long, long story of the giant maple and all it had seen in one hundred years.

"Our story and the fragrant smoke of sweet grass have made these bears calm and peaceful. Indeed, they are asleep," Grandmother said.

The bears snored on through the gnawing hunger of winter and early spring, dreaming of maple sugar.

"Our story has made these bears calm and peaceful. Indeed, they are asleep," Grandmother said.

6

Bears Make Rock Soup

Soft and deep as sleep, winter came upon the Earth. Grandmother dreamed with bears. She followed them through their sleep and talked with them in their secret snoring language. Bears told Grandmother where to find food and medicine: which roots to dig, which leaves to pick, and where the bees made honey.

Grandmother showed girls where to search beneath the snow for food. They found a mouse nest with a hidden treasure: dried-up kernels of corn; dried-up beans, nuts and seeds; even bits of roots and mushrooms—a perfect soup mix. "Thank you, Mouse, for leaving us this gift."

Women gathered wood to keep the fire burning and brought out baskets of good things they had been saving—corn, squash, and beans. Girls put food into the kettle. Bears added rocks to the soup. "Rocks are the bones of the earth," said Grandmother. "They hold mysterious life."

"We will offer prayers and food to honor our animal helpers," Grandmother said. She gathered the little ones around her. It snowed and snowed. And bears made rock soup.

Bears added rocks to the soup. "Rocks are the bones of the earth," said Grandmother.

Bears Return the Lost Children

Bears found the lost children and carried them home.

One winter two little children wandered off in a fever. They were very sick. Soon it would be dark, and then Owl would get them. Women of the family called upon bears to bring the children back.

The children wandered a long time in the snow until they got so tired they lay down. They no longer felt cold. They could no longer move their arms and legs. They were frozen.

Many strange, spotted people walked by, coughing. The children tried to call out, but they had lost their voices. Then they knew these people were ghosts.

Bears, who sometimes roam the edge of the spirit world, found these children before the spotted ghosts could take them. The huge, warm, furry bears grabbed up the children and carried them safely home.

The Naming Ceremony

A child was born! The Deer Clan welcomed their sacred gift. The family held a gathering to celebrate and give the child a name.

Aunties made a cradleboard to carry him safely through the first two years of his life. They beaded it with beautiful designs so that the Creator would smile upon this baby. Grandmothers made a feast and bathed their baby boy in the sweet smoke of cedar.

A wise old person was invited to give the boy his first name. People would not speak his name carelessly. They would use his name sparingly, so that it would stay strong all his life.

When he became a man and accomplished a great deed, he earned a new honor name which no one would know unless he wished them to.

He became a great hunter, warrior, and helper of his people. He was known as Deer Chief.

A child was born! The Deer Clan welcomed their sacred gift.

The Abandoned Yearling

Springtime came, and Yearling Moose had gotten tall and lanky. He was awkward, moody, and always in the way. He bumped about aimlessly while his mother looked for food. Suddenly, his mother ran at him and struck him with her hooves, chasing him away.

Yearling didn't know that soon his mother would be having twins. It was time for her to raise them and be done with him. It was time for him to learn how to be a big, strong, bull moose on his own.

Yearling only knew that his mother had abandoned him. He did not understand why. He stood by his lonesome self, crying for someone to take care of him.

Children saw Yearling crying and felt sorry for him. They led him to a tipi, where women warmed him with a robe and fed him. They explained how every yearling moose must leave its mother and make its way in the world.

Other young moose called to him, "Join us! Join us!" And he did.

Yearling Moose only knew that his mother had abandoned him. He did not understand why.

Grandfather Moose

Grandfather Moose had lived to a wise and powerful age. His grandchildren were numerous. And yet he wandered through the woods, looking for… something. He waded into a lake, chewing thoughtfully on a water rush. Then he remembered what he was looking for.

Grandfather Moose emerged and went to the place where he was born. He found the Moose Clan women who had helped him when he was a cold, abandoned yearling. "I have come to commission a magnificent robe," he announced. "Only you can make one that is fit to warm a great old bull moose like me."

The women sang to Grandfather Moose as they worked on his robe. He was pleased to hear their words. They sang about his many brave deeds and all the cold hard winters he had lived through. They sang about the great distances he had wandered, always looking for his mother, the Earth, to whom he would finally return.

Grandfather Moose began to feel warm and happy. He thanked the women for their song. He gave them a handsome gift—the "moose track" pattern on the magnificent robe, which he left behind for these women.

Then he wandered off into his old age.

The women sang to Grandfather Moose as they worked on his robe.

Forest of the Deer Spirits

Deer Clan women traveled across the prairie to get firewood. They followed a little creek down into a wooded hollow. They saw many tracks of leaping deer as they went, but they could not see what had startled the deer.

The women quickly gathered the wood. As they hurried to leave, a terrible storm arose. They had to turn back into the shelter of the hollow. The blizzard whipped above them, but the hollow was still and calm.

The women kept watch. They heard a faint and haunting music as the wind blew through the trees. Suddenly, they saw deer spirits leaping higher and higher, to the tops of the trees. Then the women knew what haunted this hollow. Too many hunters had taken the bodies of the deer and left in a hurry, without giving thanks to the Creator. The deer spirits were trapped here.

"Deer! We will help you get away," called the women. They sang and made healing smoke rise above the trees. The deer leaped into the smoke and disappeared into the spirit world where they belonged.

Suddenly, they saw deer spirits leaping higher and higher, to the tops of the trees.

Lisa A. Fifield 1998 ©

Broken-Winged Dance
of the Loon Clan Women

The speed of Loon in the water was unmatched, but when she was on the shore, she was so clumsy she could hardly walk. Even so, Loon had the strongest heart of any bird. She showed the other birds how to fool their enemies with bravery.

One day, Panther approached Loon's nest. Loon saw Panther and flapped crazily about, as if her wings were broken. Panther thought Loon was an easy meal. He forgot all about the nest and chased Loon instead. But before Panther could catch her, Loon dove into the water. Then she came up and laughed her wild, taunting laugh. She did this over and over, tormenting her enemy to exhaustion.

Every year Loon flew south to spend a warmer winter. Before she came back home, women of the Loon Clan would go down into the lake to perform a sacred dance. Their dance honored Loon's bravery, and reminded the waterbirds to return to the north to build their nests and make new life.

Women of the Loon Clan performed a sacred dance honoring Loon's bravery.

21

Sky Chief and His Children

Sky Chief is like a giant eagle. Some know him as Thunderbird, the messenger of the Creator. His voice is the first gigantic *crack!* of thunder in a storm, and his flashing eyes are the lightning.

When the world was still new, a flood covered the land and the People ran for high ground. Sky Chief plucked four Eagle Clan women from a mountain. He brought them to his nest up in the clouds. They cared for his children, feeding them fish and animals that Sky Chief would drop to them each time he passed by.

Sky Chief brought four Eagle Clan women to his nest up in the clouds.

From that time on, Sky Chief looked kindly upon the People. He made rain so that the grass and the buffalo could live. In that way, the People could live too.

Sky Chief's children now rule the four directions. They see the People down below and heed their messages. That is why the People, when they want to reach the Creator, send smoke and prayers up to the sky.

Keepers of the Sky

A family of hunters went out on the prairie. In the distance they saw an enemy war party coming on horseback.

The hunters were on foot. They sneaked through the grass into a big marsh. Thousands upon thousands of ducks, geese, and other waterbirds covered the marsh, but not one bird flapped or squawked to give away the hunters' hiding place.

The war party came looking for the hunters. They rode down upon the marsh. A great noise started among the waterbirds. They rose and stirred up the sky, blinding the enemy, even blocking the sun. The Canada geese were the last birds to fly away.

Once again the marsh was still. The war party searched for signs of the hunters. They surrounded the marsh. They waited for the hunters to try to get out.

Morning came and still the family of hunters was nowhere to be found. The war party knew then that these hunters had strong medicine from above. They had flown away with the Canada geese, who are the keepers of the sky.

The hunters had flown away with the keepers of the sky.

Crows Cawed a Warning

It was wartime, and there was danger all around. Soldiers were chasing the People across the territory. The People were hungry, but they could not stop to hunt because the soldiers might catch up to them. The People had to keep moving so they could cross the border and escape into Canada, where the soldiers could not follow.

The People were safe. Crows had ruined the attack.

Deer Chief led his people toward the border as the sky grew light one morning. They didn't know that the enemy was almost upon them, getting ready to attack.

Caw! Caw! Caw! A sudden explosion of crows filled the sky, warning the People that danger was near. The People hurried across the border. The enemy soldiers came chasing after them, but it was too late. The People were safe. Crows had ruined the attack.

Across the border, the People found buffalo and a good place to camp. There was a great feast and celebration to which the crows were welcomed. To this day, it is considered polite to leave a morsel of food and something shiny for Crow. And to this day, Crow makes camp with People.

Last Respects

Deer Chief remained behind in the battle where crows saved the People. He held back the enemy soldiers so the People could get away. He fought long and hard. At last, he fell. Yet Deer Chief was not alone. All the bird and animal spirits came to the place where he laid down his life.

Bear and Wolf came to help Deer Chief on his way to the other world because Deer Chief was a great man. Moose came because Deer Chief was vigilant and wary of danger, like a moose, which is the hardest animal of all to hunt. Deer, Elk, and Antelope came because Deer Chief was as fleet of foot and noble-looking as any one among them.

Eagle came to soar with a spirit as fierce and sharp-eyed as his. Canada Goose came because the heart of Deer Chief was as faithful and true as his. Loon came because the heart of Deer Chief was just as brave and strong and free as hers.

Squirrel, Rabbit, Raccoon, and Turkey came because Deer Chief was kind and generous to all, even the small and the weak and the poor, and the foolish ones too.

In this way Deer Chief was paid his last respects.

All the bird and animal spirits came to the place where Deer Chief laid down his life.

29

Nest

A young woman went to fetch water for her family. By the lake she found some broken nests of the waterbirds. She took home the orphaned hatchlings.

She made a new nest for them and cared for them with love. She spoke to the birds and offered encouragement. She fed them with brave dreams. She sang a song to lift their spirits.

She said, "I will be your mother."

People saw this and learned from her example. They learned they must always be kind to young ones and help their spirits grow. Everyone in the Indian village was to help and teach the children. In turn, the children would grow up to be generous and good to others, and Earth would prosper.

The nest is our home, our Earth. We share it with all creatures. Because of this there is always hope—and life continues.

She made a new nest for the baby birds and cared for them with love.

Nest Series ·?·   Lisa Fifield
                                                    1/1996

THE ANIMALS IN THIS BOOK still live on the plains and in the woodlands today. **Black bears** are the most numerous species of bear in North America. They hibernate in underground dens, hollow logs, rock caves, and dense brush. **Deer** are quick, cautious animals that live in forests, fields, and swamps all over North America. **Moose** are the largest member of the deer family. They roam the northern forests of the United States (including Alaska) and Canada. **Loons** love the lakes and marshes of Michigan, Wisconsin, Minnesota, and the New England states. In winter they migrate south to the warmer Atlantic and Pacific coasts. **Crows** are mischievous, raucous, and very intelligent. They can be found almost anywhere people make their home.

Lisa Fifield is a renowned watercolorist and quiltmaker. She is of Native American and German descent and is enrolled in the Oneida Tribe of Indians of Wisconsin, which is one of the Five Nations of the Iroquois Confederacy. Her award-winning art-work expresses her history, culture, and experience as a Native American woman. Lisa's paintings have been exhibited in museums and galleries around the world.

For my.mom, who dedicated herself to her children. For my dad, who believed in the wonder of childhood. For my son Ryan, my sisters and brothers, and Dr. Jerome Dougan. Thanks to my friends Lee Brooks and Susan Eyerly.
—Lisa Fifield

Lise Erdrich is a counselor and health educator at the Circle of Nations Indian School in Wahpeton, North Dakota. She is of Native American and German descent and is enrolled in the Turtle Mountain Band of Plains Ojibway. Her grandfather, a tribal leader and historian, encouraged her interest in writing and in the Ojibway language and culture. Lise's writing has appeared in literary magazines and anthologies.

With great big bear hugs for my wee lads Justin, Jake, and Levi, and special thanks to our best friend Taz. He is always there for us with love, support, and devotion, and a kindly wag of his tail.
—Lise Erdrich

Library of Congress Cataloging-in-Publication Data

Erdrich, Lise.
Bears make rock soup and other stories / paintings by Lisa Fifield; stories by Lise Erdrich.
    p. cm.
Summary: A collection of stories inspired by paintings that depict the special relationships between the plains and woodland Indians and such animals as bear, deer, moose, crows, and loons.
    ISBN 0-89239-172-3
1. Indians of North America—Great Plains—Juvenile fiction. 2. Children's stories, American. [1. Indians of North America—Great Plains—Fiction. 2. Animals—Fiction. 3. Short stories.] I. Fifield, Lisa, ill. II. Title.

PZ7.E72553 Be 2002
[E]—dc21

2001042461

Paintings copyright ©2002 by Lisa Fifield
Stories copyright ©2002 by Lise Erdrich

Senior Editor: Harriet Rohmer
Assistant Editor: Dana Goldberg
Consulting Editors: Ina Cumpiano, David Schecter
Design and Production: Katherine Tillotson
Special thanks to Betty Berenson

Distributed to the book trade by Publishers Group West. Quantity discounts are available through the publisher for educational and nonprofit use.

Printed in Hong Kong through Marwin Productions
10 9 8 7 6 5 4 3 2

Children's Book Press is a nonprofit publisher of multicultural literature for children, supported in part by grants from the California Arts Council. Write us for a complimentary catalog: Children's Book Press, 2211 Mission Street, San Francisco, CA 94110   (415) 821-3080
Visit our website at www.childrensbookpress.org.